D0502347

By_____

ACCOLADES FOR THE
ALDO ZELNICK COMIC NOVEL SERIES

An alphabetical adventure for middle-grade readers 7 to 13

Book of the Year Award, juvenile fiction, *ForeWord Reviews*

Colorado Book Award, juvenile literature

Mountains & Plains Independent Booksellers
Association Regional Book Award

Creative Child magazine Seal of Excellence

Kids' Next Indiebound selection

Independent Publisher Silver "IPPY" Award

Creative Child magazine Preferred Choice Award

Quid Novi Award, first prize

Moonbeam Children's Book Award,
silver medal for comic/graphic novel

Top 10 Educational Children's Products - Dr. Toy

Book of the Year Award, kids' fiction,
Creative Child magazine

Moonbeam Children's Book Award,
silver medal for activity book

Ignoramus

AN ALDO ZELNICK COMIC NOVEL

Written by Karla Oceanak

Illustrated by Kendra Spanjer

BAILIWICK PRESS

Also by Karla Oceanak
and Kendra Spanjer –
Artsy-Fartsy, Bogus, Cahoots,
Dumbstruck, Egghead,
Finicky, Glitch, Hotdogger,
All Me, All the Time

Published by:
Bailiwick Press
309 East Mulberry Street
Fort Collins, Colorado 80524
(970) 672-4878
Fax: (970) 672-4731
www.bailiwickpress.com
www.aldozelnick.com

Manufactured by:
Friesens Corporation, Altona, Canada
October 2013
Job # 89676

Book design by:
Launie Parry
Red Letter Creative
www.red-letter-creative.com

ISBN 978-1-934649-41-1

22 21 20 19 18 17 16 15 14 13   7 6 5 4 3 2 1

Dear Aldo—

Happy Valentine's month to my darling Valentine!

xx Goosy

ALDO,

A Valentine inscription,* in the immortal* words of W. Shakespeare:

"Love looks not with the eyes, but with the mind.

"And therefore is winged Cupid painted blind."

– Mr. Mot

WHO'S WHO

My main men:

Danny

Jack, my bestie.

Me – Aldo Valentine Zelnick. Gah!

Marvin

Tommy Geller

Mr. Fodder, my cafeteria guy, and his dog, Greta.

Grover

My friends-who-are-girls, Bee and Iyla.

Emilio

8

MY BROTHER, TIMOTHY, AND HIS (EW) GIRLFRIEND, SASHA.

MOM, DAD, AND OUR DOG, MAX.

JACK'S DAD, FRITZ, AND HIS GIRLFRIEND, HAZEL.

MY GRANDMA, GOOSY.

JACK'S MOM, MRS. LOPEZ, AND JACK'S GRANDPA, ABUELO.

MRS. DULCET, MY BAND TEACHER.

MR. MOT, BOOK NERD.

9

Hi. My name's Bee. My inventive* friend Aldo Zelnick makes these sketchbooks. And he let ME help make the one you're holding!

When you see *, you're in luck! It means you can look in the back of the book to see what the word means!

TWANG!!!

Every kid who reads these books falls in love with them, but I shot them just in case.

10

THE DAY THAT WILL LIVE IN INFAMY*

How come everyone loves YOU so much?

To tell you the truth, I think it's the chocolates. Plus I'm short. People love short.

JANUARY

FEBRUARY 14

I'd like to start my I sketchbook with a question for the Guy in charge of the getting-born schedule:

WHY, WHY, WHY DID MY BIRTHDAY HAVE TO BE FEBRUARY 14TH???

It causes infinite* humiliation! Such as: My birthday presents get wrapped in frilly pink and red. My parents picked Valentine for my middle name. And my mom sends little packaged heart cakes to school for my class birthday treat.

Sigh.

It's not February's fault, but the month is basically a total loss because of dumb Valentine's Day. The second the calendar flips past January,

11

bam—everything turns from humdrum to lovey-dovey, and my birthday gets infected* by mush.

Already this morning, even though it's only February 2nd, the tragedy of my birth date embarrassed me in band class. I was just sitting there with my trumpet, minding my own spit valve, when Jack loud-whispered to me:

EVERYONE THINKS YOU'RE A SAINT, VALENTINE, BUT YOU'RE NOT FOOLING ME—YOU'RE A BIRTHDAY-WRECKER!

HEY, ALDO, WHAT'S THE PLAN FOR YOUR BIRTHDAY PARTY THIS YEAR?

NOT SURE. I WAS THINKING PIZZA—PEPPERONI AND ONION...

NO! I MEAN, WHAT ARE WE GONNA DO?

OH. LASER TAG? IRON MAN MARATHON?

Our band teacher, Mrs. Dulcet, was busy passing out new sheet music. When she finished, she stepped back up onto her standing box at the front of the room and said, "In honor of Valentine's Day, I've chosen an '80s pop tune called 'Dancing with Myself,' written and made famous by punk rocker Billy Idol."

From the percussion section shot up Bee's hand. (Surprise, surprise.) She's my neighbor and friend-who-happens-to-be-a-girl. "'Dancing with Myself' doesn't sound very romantic," she said.

"On the contrary," replied Mrs. Dulcet. "This is a song about the reality of romance, which is that many people find themselves alone on Valentine's Day..." Her voice trailed off like she started thinking about bacon or something.

"Aw geez, here we go...," I muttered—just loud enough to be heard, apparently. (Note to self: work on muttering volume.)

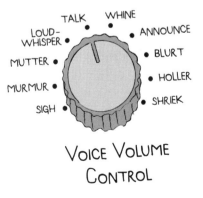

VOICE VOLUME CONTROL

13

DO YOU HAVE A THOUGHT TO SHARE WITH THE CLASS, MR. ZELNICK?

I shook my head no, but Mrs. Dulcet did not let it drop. "So do _you_ look forward to Valentine's Day?" she interrogated* me. _Me._ Why do I get all the weird teacher questions?

"Ummm...," I started to say.

That's when Jack jumped in. He's my best friend, and he was just trying to save me from the awkwardness, but he only made things awkwarder.

"Aldo _loves_ Valentine's Day!" he hollered. "Because it's his birthday! His middle name is even Valentine!"

14

The entire 5th grade band launched into a symphony of laughter. And my face got hotter

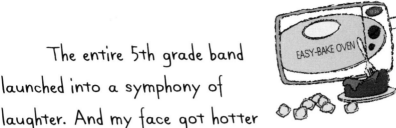

than the Easy-Bake Oven I got for my birthday when I was 5. (What?! It made cake! And pizza bites!)

Mrs. Dulcet winked at me. "I guess Aldo is one of the fortunate few who will never be lonely on Valentine's Day," she said.

After band, I stopped at the water fountain on the way to lunch to spray my oven-face with cold water. Jack and Bee caught up to me.

WELL HELLO, ALDO VALENTINE ZELNICK.

SORRY 'BOUT THAT, DUDE.

SURELY THIS DAY CAN'T GET ANY WORSE.

15

"I didn't know your birthday was in February," said Bee. "I'm excited to come to your party!"

"You're a girl," I reminded her.

"So? You can have a boy-girl party!" said Bee. "A boy-girl Valentine's party! It's perfect!"

"That's gonna be a no."

Bee just smiled her Beeish smile.

Then at the end of the afternoon, my teacher, Mr. Krug, stood at the front of the classroom with a pink sheet of paper. "This is a list of all the students in this class," he said. "I'm sending it home with you today, in your Monday folders. It'll come in handy when you start writing out Valentines for the class party, which is a week from Friday."

Blerg.

OK, maybe I can't control the mushification of February, but this year I will not let my birthday get infiltrated* by Valentine's Day! There will be no pink. No hearts. No lace. No girls. And no dancing! Sheesh. A boy's gotta stand up for his boy rights, even if his middle name is, unfortunately, Valentine.

CH·SMOOCH·SM

IF ONLY EVERY KIND OF KISS WAS AS INNOCUOUS* AND TASTY AS THESE BABIES

THE KISS

If you don't count the fact that Marvin Shoemaker has started to call me Val, I made it through the whole school day today without hearing about Valentine's Day even once. It was a February miracle!

When I got home from school, I plopped down on the couch to watch me some History Channel. I must have fallen asleep, because I woke up to the sounds of my mom and dad chatting and banging pots around in the kitchen. Dinnertime. And, I realized as I slowly overcame the inertia* of sleep and returned to reality, they were talking about my birthday present!

HE REALLY WANTED AN ELECTRIC SCOOTER AT CHRISTMAS, REMEMBER?

OH YES. AND ALSO A SNOW-CONE CART.

OH BE STILL, MY BEATING HEART!

I ♥ NY

6:06

AND I'D LIKE A PET CAT. TO CHASE.

18

Hope began to float up inside me like a helium bubble. For my birthday, I was going to get the incredible* presents I'd asked for at Christmas but hadn't gotten! What a great parenting strategy! Mom and Dad had just been teaching me to be patient and persistent and all that bologna!

But a second later my hope bubble burst... because my parents started laughing. This went on for some time.

"Really, though," said Mom at last, sighing as she finally recovered from the hysterics. "What do you think he wants for his birthday?"

"I don't know. But I do know what I want right now," said Dad, his voice growly with innuendo.* "An appetizer kiss."

Followed by a mom-giggle and wet mouth noises.

"Ewww!" I announced, jumping up from my hiding spot. "Gross! You're making me lose my appetite! And you're gonna get spit in my food!"

Mom jumped and hollered too. "Aldo! You scared me half to death!"

"Gathering a little birthday present intelligence* there, were you, sport?" said Dad.

"No! I wasn't spying! I fell asleep! And then you woke me up with your slobbering! Ew!" I stopped exclaiming for a second to shake off my heebie-jeebies. "I'm not even 11 yet, remember? PG-13 behavior when I'm in the room is <u>not</u> <u>appropriate</u>!"

Mom rolled her eyes. "I'll remember that the next time you want to watch *Iron Man*. Now let's talk about your birthday. Do you have any presents on your wish list?" She handed me a long carrot rolled up in a leaf of iceberg lettuce* and squirted some Italian dressing into a bowl.

IS THIS SOME KIND OF A SPRING ROLL...?

SOMETHING LIKE THAT.

I dipped and crunched. "Welp, I was thinking my own laptop computer would be useful..."

Again the eye roll. "What about a party?" she said.

"Oh yeah. I did want to talk to you about that. This year can we please have no Valentine's stuff of any kind? No pink, no hearts, no nothing like that?"

"Fair enough. What's on the itinerary* then?"

"Something dude-ish, like laser tag or a pellet-gun fight. Then pizza and video games. And a sleepover, of course."

"Sounds doable," said Dad as he drained the spaghetti noodles. "Now please set the table and tell Timothy it's time to eat."

Spaghetti and garlic bread—yorm! But hey! I just realized I was tricked into enjoying a salad! That mother of mine... One minute she's getting germs all over your food, and the next she's hoodwinking you into eating vegetables disguised as a burrito. She can't be trusted, I tell ya.

21

EYES ON THE PRIZE

Bee thinks she's so wonderful. In band today, Mrs. Dulcet was all, "Nice work on that tricky snare passage, Bee," and Bee was all, "Thanks, Mrs. Dulcet. I've been working on it."

So at lunch I felt it was my obligation to remind Bee that the snare drum is not a <u>real</u> instrument. "You basically just bang on an ice-cream pail with a couple of sticks," I said.

"The drums are not easy," she said. "I practice a lot! And I take private lessons."

"Pffft. From a baby?"

YOU WISH...

I TAUGHT RINGO EVERYTHING HE KNOWS.

She scowled. "Sometimes you are so irksome,* Aldo. The trumpet is easier than the drums. Actually, I bet you I can play the trumpet better than you can."

EVERYONE KNOWS DRUMS ARE THE IN-THING.*

OH YEAH? WELL HOW COME NOBODY SINGS ALONG TO YOUR PART?

"Nuh-uh. Wait—have you been taking trumpet lessons too?"

"Nope. I've never played the trumpet before, not even once. But Friday in band class I'll prove to you how easy it is. Let's make it a contest. Winner gets to choose the prize."

"OK. You're on!"

23

What prize should I demand when I win? I could have Bee carry my backpack to and from school for a month. Or if the snow in my back yard ever melts, she could do my poop-scooping chore! Or whoa...maybe I could get free pizza from her family's restaurant... So many possibilities! I'll have to give it some thought.

I'm supposed to practice my trumpet 15 minutes a day, and tonight I might even do it. But first I'm gonna go sneak Timothy's iPhone and play some Inkvaders...

24

BORROWERS' CLUB

MR. MOT'S LIBRARY

Somehow the little man in Inkvaders reminded me of my teacher, Mr. Krug, which reminded me that Mr. Krug assigned us a book report, which reminded me that the book report is due next week, which reminded me that I hadn't even picked a book yet. So I did what I always do when I need something new to read—I went to see my retired English teacher neighbor, Mr. Mot. He's like a walking, talking book app. And his house, which has a bajillion shelves chock-full of books, is like my private library.

I knocked on his front door, right below this weird little sign that says:

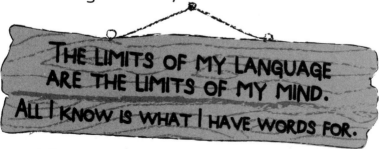

THE LIMITS OF MY LANGUAGE ARE THE LIMITS OF MY MIND. ALL I KNOW IS WHAT I HAVE WORDS FOR.

Whatever that means.

25

I LIKE BIG BOOKS AND I CANNOT LIE.

"February salutations, my young friend!" he said when he opened the door. "Why, if I'm not mistaken, you have a birthday approaching!"

"Yup. I'm gonna be 11."

"An auspicious age! Come in, come in! Of what service may I be on this cold winter's night?"

"I need a book."

"Ahhh. You have found me in the midst of rereading Homer's epic poem the Iliad.* Perhaps you would care to join me?"

"Perhaps not. I'm allergic to poems, especially long ones. I need a kid book."

So we went to his shelves, and I climbed his rolling ladder dealie. He gave me a ride over to the kid book section.

TALES   CHILDREN'S
ENCYCLOPEDIAS
SHAKESPEARE
ETRY   MORE BORING STUFF
COMICS

MY COLLECTION IS OUTGROWING ITS ACCOMMODATIONS! I MAY HAVE TO CONVERT TO E-BOOKS.

DON'T DO THAT! ONLY REAL BOOKS NEED REAL LADDERS!

"What sort of a tale strikes your fancy? Scintillating science fiction? Intrepid* history? Epic fantasy? Or, in honor of the approaching holiday, a touch of romance?"

"No! No romance!" I said. "I'm ignoring* Valentine's Day. This year, February 14th is just gonna be my birthday. How about something with battles and blood?"

27

Mr. Mot nodded gravely. "A masculine tale, then. Yes, yes, here is something of that ilk*: *The Indian in the Cupboard.*"

On the book's cover stood a muscle-y, mad-looking Indian with 2 big feathers sticking out of the top of his head and holding a bow and arrow. Next to him was a cowboy in yellow pants shooting a pistol.

"Guys. Weapons. Perfectamundo," I said.

Just then came another knock at Mr. Mot's front door, and in walked...Mrs. Dulcet!

"Well hello, Aldo!" she said. "Fancy meeting you here!" She raised her eyebrows and looked at Mr. Mot, who *ahemed.*

28

"I see no introductions are necessary," he said as he walked around behind me and placed his hands on my shoulders. "And the hour grows late for a young man on a school night," he added as he steered me toward the door, "so I bid you adieu, Aldo. Please do let me know what you think of the novel..."

And with that, he practically pushed me outside, into the cold, dark night.

I walked back home with a book in my hand and a question in my brain. Why would Mrs. Dulcet be at Mr. Mot's house? She's a Mrs., and old people don't do stuff after dark, anyway. But he <u>does</u> play guitar, and she's a music teacher... Maybe he's taking lessons?

I HAVE A QUESTION IN MY BRAIN TOO. WHEN'S <u>MY</u> BIRTHDAY?

29

3 DUMB THINGS

Even though it's just February 6th,
3 Valentiney things happened at school today:

1. First thing this morning,
my art teacher, Ms. Munroe,
showed us a famous painting
"in honor of Valentine's
Day." It's called *The Kiss*,
and it's by some dead artist
from Austria named
Gus Klimt.

BLECH!
NOT COOL!

Lovey-dovey
art at 8:30
a.m.—it's enough
to make a person

PRETTY COOL

lose his Lucky Charms. But if you squint your
eyes to blur out the mushiness, it's a super-cool
painting. Klimt used awesome shapes, bright colors,
and even real gold tinfoil on top of the paint!

30

"Klimt's father was a gold engraver," explained Ms. Munroe, "which may be how he thought to apply gold to his paintings during what we now call his 'Golden Period.' He focused on women and relationships in his art."

What a waste of talent. And expensive metal.

Then Ms. Munroe us make our own drawings of the painting by looking at it on her smartboard and mimicking it as good as we could. She had Danny stand up to show us his copy. It was just OK, but all the girls in the class oohed and aahed like he was Klimt Junior.

Puhleez.

DON'T IDOLIZE* ME FOR MY LOOKS, GIRLS. IDOLIZE ME FOR MY ARTISTIC ABILITIES.

I'M NOT IRISH, BUT KISS ME ANYWAY

31

(2.) In Language Arts, like usual, Mr. Krug had us pair up with someone to work on our Idioms* of the Week worksheet. This gave Jack and me a chance to talk more about my birthday party.

WHO SHOULD I INVITE BESIDES YOU?

I'M INVITED? OH GOOD.

"Danny. Tommy Geller. Maybe Grover?" suggested Jack.

Grover's our class rich kid. "Hm. I've never invited him before, but I bet he gives insanely* good presents."

Jack was filling in the worksheet section about the saying "eat crow." (Apparently when you "eat crow," you don't actually eat a gross black bird. It means you were wrong about something and now you have to admit it and say you're sorry. Weird.)

He slid me the worksheet. "Here. You're the artsy-fartsy one. You draw the crow."

32

Mr. Krug makes us write about <u>and</u> draw the sayings on our Idioms of the Week worksheets. He says it helps us remember them.

EATING CROW

YOU'RE RIGHT, ALDO. I WAS WRONG. YOU'RE A <u>MUCH</u> BETTER TRUMPET PLAYER THAN I AM!

Jack watched me draw. "Are you gonna invite Bee to your party?" he asked. "I mean, she's our friend..."

"It's a boy party! Plus, Bee would be the only girl there. Don't you think that'd be awkward for her?"

I finished the drawing and flipped the worksheet to the last Idiom of the Week: birthday suit.

Right about then Mr. Krug called out, "Oh! And you don't need to draw a picture of the idiom on the back of today's worksheet! Just define what it means and use it in a sentence!"

Pockets of giggles broke out here and there. I shoved the worksheet back at Jack.

He grinned. "Are you gonna wear your birthday suit at your birthday party?" he said—a little too blurty. The class's giggles increased* to guffaws.

MY BIRTHDAY SUIT. AT LEAST IT STILL FITS.

3. When Jack and I walked home from school, we stopped at his dad-house because Jack's staying there tonight. Timothy's girlfriend, Sasha, lives next door to Jack's dad.

And guess what we saw on Sasha's front porch, in broad daylight? Timothy and Sasha wrapped around each other in a hug like a piece of Twizzler.

"Knock it off!" I yelled at Timothy.

His reply came in the form of a snowball to my cranium.

OK, that's it. I'm so done with this whole Valentine's Day thing. I've made some cards to hand to people when they infringe* on my rights to experience a non-romantic February:

PUBLIC DISPLAYS OF AFFECTION ARE AN INVASION OF MY PRIVACY.

ROMANTIC = NO, CRAM IT

FEBRUARY IS FOR PRESIDENTS.

I HAVE A SEVERE SALIVA ALLERGY.

PLEASE— NO KISSING IN MY PRESENCE.

FRIENDS DON'T LET FRIENDS SEND VALENTINES.

POW! BE A FIGHTER, NOT A LOVER.

35

BACON • BOY

IN Be a Fighter, not a Lover

VALENTINE'S DAY, SCHMALENTINE'S DAY.

YEAH, LIKE SAVING THE WORLD.

WE'VE GOT IMPORTANT STUFF TO WORRY ABOUT!

FEAST ON THIS, VORACIO!

CHOCOLATE SHOP

YOU STUPID CHOCOLATES ARE SO MELTY!!!

WHY COULDN'T I HAVE BEEN BORN A BROCCOLI?!

WHOA, LETTUCE LADY, I NEVER KNEW YOU HAD LASER EYES...

LEAF ME ALOOONE!

YOU ARE ONE INCREDIBLE EDIBLE!

I DO WHAT I CAN.

OH C'MON. SERIOUSLY? WHAT DID I JUST SAY?

SMOOCH SMOOCH SMOOCH SMOOCH SMOOCH

UGH. SALAD IS ICKY.

HAPPY V DAY, BACON BOY.

UH, I MUSTA FORGOTTEN YOUR CARD AT HOME. I'VE BEEN KINDA BUSY...

THERE'S NO CARD.

Cream

INTOLERABLE*!

Mwah ha ha ha!

I'm so horrified I can barely hold a pencil.

Today in band class Abigail Goode (that's Bee) tricked me into losing our instrument play-off. Here's what happened.

The second I walked into the band room, she pounced on me. "Time for our contest!" she chirped.

"Uh..." See, the thing is, I'd forgotten all about it.

She handed me her drumsticks, and she snatched my trumpet case from my hand.

"Hey!" I protested. I hadn't practiced my own instrument, let alone hers.

38

"Mrs. Dulcet agreed to judge," said Bee. "We're just going to play the first few bars of each of our parts in 'Dancing with Myself.' Do you want to go first or should I?"

"I'm not ready! I've been kinda busy..."

"I'll take that as a 'Bee, you go first.'" And she sat down, put her lips on my mouthpiece, and perfectly played my trumpet.

"You cheated!"

"No I didn't. I just borrowed a school trumpet for a couple days and did this little thing called practicing. You should try it sometime. Your turn," she added, motioning for me to sit down in the chair and placing the drum sheet music on the stand.

Uh-oh, I realized right away. Drum music looks a lot different than trumpet music.

DRUM/WEIRDO MUSIC:

Xs AND RECTANGLES?! THE ONLY REAL NOTES ARE ON THE SAME LINE! HOW ARE YOU SUPPOSED TO PLAY WITH TWO HANDS? WHAT IS THIS?

TRUMPET/NORMAL MUSIC:

39

I tapped the drum a couple times then realized I had no idea what was going on. I shrugged and, for the second time this week in band class, my face got inferno* hot.

"Better luck next time, Aldo!" was all Mrs. Dulcet said.

"For my prize, I want an invitation to your birthday party," Bee said right away.

I shook my head. Nosirree.

OH C'MON, ALDO! I WON'T BE GIRLY...I PROMISE! DANNY'S GOING, RIGHT? MAYBE WE COULD PLAY TWISTER! PLEEEASE?!

NO WAY. PICK SOMETHING ELSE.

40

At my feet sat my backpack, and when Bee looked down, she noticed a tan-colored book corner peeking out of the top of it.

"OK then," she said. "If I'm not getting invited to your party, my second choice is being co-creator of your I sketchbook."

"No can do."

"Aldo," said Bee sternly. "We agreed that the winner got to choose the prize. I don't even have to give you 2 options, but I am, because I'm nice. So which will it be?" And she crossed her arms across her chest and raised an eyebrow.

BEE AT MY PARTY? OR BEE IN MY SKETCBOOK?

A SLEEPOVER'S NOT A SLEEPOVER WITHOUT BEAUTY PARLOR TIME!!!

OH SHOOT, I BROKE MY PINK PENCIL DRAWING ALL THESE FLOWERS!

SILLY ME, ALL THESE PENCILS ARE PINK!

By now Mrs. Dulcet was telling everyone to sit down and start warming up. I had to decide, and fast. Both options were inconceivable*! But, I remembered, Bee <u>has</u> drawn in my sketchbooks a few times before, and she's a decent artist. Also, sharing the sketchbook with her for a whole month would be appalling...but not as appalling as having a boy-girl birthday party.

"All right already! I'll give it to you tomorrow morning. Sheesh."

So tomorrow before Spanish class I have to hand over this sketchbook to Bee. So she can touch it. And draw in it. And generally girl it up.

BEE DREW IN ARTSY-FARTSY, TOO, AND IT JUST ABOUT DROVE ME INSANE, REMEMBER?

Adios, mi amigo libro. (In case your Spanish skills aren't as exceptional as mine, that means "Goodbye, my friend book." I think it might also mean "Goodbye, my free friend." Weird. Anyways...)

42

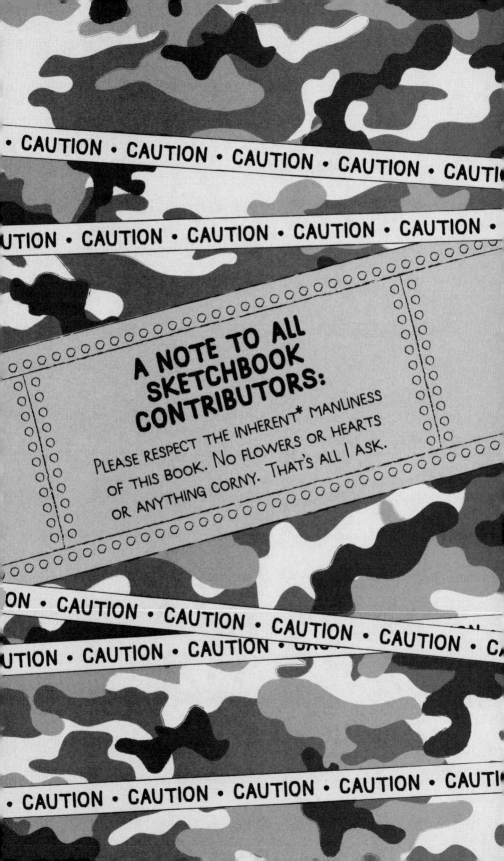

CAUTION • CAUTION • CAUTION • CAUTION • CAUTI

UTION • CAUTION • CAUTION • CAUTION • CAUTION •

A NOTE TO ALL SKETCHBOOK CONTRIBUTORS:

PLEASE RESPECT THE INHERENT* MANLINESS OF THIS BOOK. NO FLOWERS OR HEARTS OR ANYTHING CORNY. THAT'S ALL I ASK.

ON • CAUTION • CAUTION • CAUTION • CAUTION • CA

UTION • CAUTION • CAUTION •

CAUTION • CAUTION • CAUTION • CAUTION • CAUTI

Unicorns & Angel Kisses

Hi! It's Bee! Remember me?

Well, here I am, at my house, in my room, writing in Aldo Zelnick's sketchbook!

I'm sitting on a purple bedspread, propped up against a fuzzy pink pillow, with my beloved stuffed unicorn at my side.

Aldo, you and I have a magical connection!

His name's Ivanhoe!

44

Tonight I've been practicing the drums and working on handmade Valentines for the class party, but I took a break so I could enjoy some time as authoress!

I don't understand why Aldo is so against Valentine's Day. He's lucky to have a wonderful family that loves him so much, even though he's a complete curmudgeon. And he has wonderful friends—like me!

Aldo was born into his wonderful family, but my parents picked me. An orphanage in Korea was my home until the day my mom and dad went to the adoption agency here in Colorado. That's when they first saw me, in a picture.

"Even though you were 6,000 miles away, we knew you belonged here with us the moment we saw your shiny black eyes and sweet dimples."

That's the story they always tell me, anyway.

When I was 7 my parents gave birth to a baby: my little sister, Vivi!

They say she's their second miracle.

So I think Valentine's Day is the best holiday in the world because it's all about celebrating the love we share with the people who care about us! And if my birthday was February 14th, I would feel like angel kisses were raining down on me!

Now if only Aldo would invite me to his birthday party. :[I really like Aldo and Danny and Jack and Tommy Geller and Danny. They're my best friends!

47

And not being invited to your best friend's birthday party is like...let's see, how can I put this so Aldo will understand...

It's like having your very favorite pizza come straight from the oven and get set all bubbly and gooey on the table in front of you...and then watching everyone else get to eat it—but not you, because for some reason that makes no sense, you're not included.

48

HERE'S MY PLAN:

When I give the sketchbook back to Aldo tomorrow morning, I'm going to tell him I want another sketchbook turn on Sunday. Being an author/illustrator* is invigorating*!

Look! My first contributions to the Word Gallery!

P.S. I don't really have a stuffed unicorn, and my bedspread is definitely not purple.

But I (do) believe in angel kisses and best friends.

49

YOU HAVE GOT TO BE KIDDING ME

I specifically told her "nothing corny" and what does she draw?! Unicorns, hearts, and angel kisses! And she's making handmade Valentines?!! I feel like my eyeballs need to be dunked in mud and scrubbed with bacon grease to wash away all that girliness.

You know what's weird, though? I didn't even know that Bee was adopted. I never thought about it much, but if you'd asked me, I would've guessed that she inherited* her blueish-black hair and tan skin from some long-lost relative or something. Huh.

I also didn't realize that Jack and the other guys and I are her best friends. Come to think of it, I never see her with any other kids... And we like her and everything. I mean...we don't like-like her. Gah! See what kinds of problems she causes?

50

But all that stuff about orphans and best friends, that's just to make me feel guilty so I'll invite her to my party. And the pizza she talked about? She can't fool me. Her parents own a <u>restaurant,</u> so she can have her favorite pizza anytime she wants it.

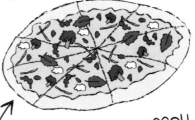

BEE'S FAVORITE: BROCCOLI, KALE, BEET SHREDS, SHRIVELED-UP MUSHROOMS, STINKY GOAT CHEESE... AND PROBABLY RAISINS

Does she think I'm idiotic* or something?

Ope...Timothy just yelled up the stairs that it's dinnertime. And <u>that</u> is one of my favorite times of the day. BRB.

At dinner my mom handed me a box of *Iron Man* valentines and a bag of Mike & Ikes.

"I picked these up at the store today. For your class Valentine's Day party," she said.

"I'll take the candy, but I'm not giving out Valentines this year."

51

"Oh Aldo. It's your last classroom Valentine's party! You won't have one next year when you're in middle school. And are you planning to accept Valentines from the other kids—and the candy that comes attached to them?"

"Well, yeah. I'm not the boss of them."

"Then you're giving out Valentines. You cannot be a taker unless you're also a giver."

"That's one of those basic rules of life, sport," said Dad.

"Yeah, Aldo <u>Valentine</u>," said Timothy.

"Yeah, Timothy <u>Karl</u>," I said.

It didn't have the same effect. So I changed the subject by bringing up my archery idea. See, I've been reading that *Indian in the Cupboard* book, and it's got me thinking that bows and arrows are pretty macho. So I asked if, for my party, we could go somewhere to shoot arrows...you know, before coming back to our house for pizza and the rest of the inevitable* messing around.

"Sounds great!" said Dad.

"I'm not sure it's a good idea," said the official family worrier, A.K.A. Mom. "Your arm is still healing, remember? I'll call the doctor and ask."

If the doctor says OK, I'm _so_ gonna rock at archery. After all, it's a sport where one of the main skills is standing perfectly still.

And now, since it's Friday night, I'm off to bed—kinda!

MR. MOT SAYS I'M INDEFATIGABLE* WHEN IT COMES TO VIDEO GAMES. THAT'S CUZ I'VE BUILT UP MY THUMB MUSCLES.

THAT'S RIGHT, I'M DOIN' THE WORM!

GETTIN' JIGGY WITH IT

This morning I walked on water. You always knew this day was coming, didn't you.

Gotcha! The water was frozen! Jack's dad took Jack and me and my mom and Goosy ice fishing.

In case you've never ice fished before, I'll tell you how it works:

YUP. IT'S EXACTLY WHAT IT SOUNDS LIKE.

1. First you go to IHOP to tank up on chicken and waffles.

2. Then you drive to a lake covered by at least 5 or 6 inches of ice. Don't forget your winter coat and snowpants and warm boots. Put all that stuff on, then walk out onto the ice.

IT SEEMS THE EVIL SNOWPANTS CAME IN HANDY AFTER ALL...

54

3. Fall down infinite times as you slip and slide your way to the middle of the lake.

4. Watch Fritz (that's Jack's dad) cut a circle hole in the ice with a giant corkscrew.

5. Hold your ice fishing pole, which is so small it looks like it's for dwarfs.

6. Wrinkle your nose because Fritz is gonna impale* a short, white worm onto your hook.

I HATE FISHING.

7. Sit on an upside-down plastic bucket and drop your wormy hook through the ice hole.

8. Jerk your fishing rod up and down a little because, irrationally,* fish like dancing food. This is called *jigging*.

I HATE FISHING.

9. Keep jigging until you feel the tug on your fishing line that means that a fish ate the worm and the hook.

55

Once Goosy and Jack and I were fishing, Fritz cut a second hole a little ways away, for him and Hazel to fish through. Oh yeah...Hazel came too. She's the ski rescue lady who helped me when I crashed and broke my arm when I was skiing last month. Ever since that fiasco, she and Fritz have been hanging out, I've noticed.

YOU'RE MANAGING JUST FINE WITH THAT CAST. YOUR MOM TOLD ME YOU CAN STILL DO YOUR HOMEWORK AND PLAY THE TRUMPET—AND VIDEO GAMES.

YEAH. IT'S NOT THAT BAD, CONSIDERING IT WAS A LIFE-THREATENING INJURY. PLUS, I ONLY HAVE TO WEAR IT FOR A FEW MORE WEEKS.

I'M PRETTY SURE I'D FIT DOWN THAT HOLE... WHAT HAPPENS IF I CATCH A BIG FISH AND HE REELS ME IN?

56

After a while I got tired of staring down the hole, so I looked around to see what else was going on. Not much. But I did see that Fritz was kneeling on the ice behind Hazel, who was sitting on a bucket as she fished. He had his arms wrapped around her, and his hands were covering hers as he showed her how to jig her line. She was giggling. I wanted to hand them one of my "Public displays of affection are an invasion of my privacy" cards, but I forgot to bring them with me. Who'd have thought I'd need them for ice fishing! Sheesh.

"So, Jack," I asked. "Is Hazel your dad's girlfriend now? Is she gonna be your new mom?"

Jack's surprised eyes flicked up at me. "What?"

I tilted my head at the Hazel-Fritz pretzel— the Fritzel. "They're stuck together like the Yu-Gi-Oh cards I spilled soda on last week."

Jack glanced at his dad. "He's just teaching her how to ice fish. I learned the same way. Duh."

"Jack, Jack, Jack. You're sooo innocent.*"

Just then Goosy let out a whoop. "I've got one! I've got one!" Her fishing rod was bent over, and something under the ice was pulling her line tight. She turned the crank to reel in whatever was playing tug of war with her, and a few seconds later, *bam*—a big gray fish with a rainbow stripe was flopping around on the ice at her feet.

Guess what's for dinner tonight?! Fresh fish cakes with lemon-dill sauce! That's my dad's fishy specialty.

In case you were wondering what my mom was doing this whole time, she didn't ice fish. She's not a sit-stiller. Instead of winter boots, she slipped on her ice skates and made girly swirls all around the lake.

58

Just a sec... I'm sitting in the fort (my bedroom closet), getting the ice-fishing day down in my sketchbook, but I just heard voices coming into my room. BRB.

Bee's here! She came to my house for the sketchbook! My mom brought her up to my room, and the two of them are sitting on my bed talking. I told them I had to finish a couple things in the sketchbook before Bee could have it, so I came back into the closet. I kept the closet door open an iota,* though, so I could hear what they're saying...

"So Aldo is sharing his sketchbook with you?" said Mom. "How nice!"

"Yes. We're switching back and forth. He wants this sketchbook to have more of a feminine point of view."

Gah! My mom loves Bee! It's because Bee speaks parentese to ingratiate* herself.

"You are really a good influence* on Aldo, Bee. It sounds like you're helping him become more considerate of what other people think and feel."

59

"Thanks, Mrs. Zelnick. I try."

Barf. Barf. Barf.

"Aldo's birthday party is next Saturday," continued Mom.

"I know!" said Bee. "He's so lucky to have his birthday on Valentine's Day!" Her voice sounded all high and excited, like a happy chipmunk. But then it dropped real low and got all sad and slow. "But...I'm not invited."

PUPPY EYES ALWAYS WORK ON ALDO'S MOM.

"Oh don't be silly. Of course you're invited!"

"Aldo said it's not a boy-girl party..."

"Well, I'll have a talk with him about that. Aldo, come out of that closet right this instant and give Bee the sketchbook! It's her turn!"

Gah. If my mom's on Bee's side, that's not good. Moms are practically impervious* to mind-changing. I'll have to come up with an ironclad* reason to keep Abigail Goode away from my party...

60

HEY. THE BUCK STOPS HERE. AND SO DO ALL THE HEARTS AND FLOWERS.

A NOTE TO ALL SKETCHBOOK CONTRIBUTORS:

READING WHAT OTHER PEOPLE WRITE IN THEIR OWN SKETCHBOOKS IS IMPOLITE.*

Ikebana!

On Sunday afternoons my mom and I sometimes go to the flower shop called Iris. It's closed on Sundays, but a friend of ours, Mr. Ishii, owns it. He meets us there to teach us ikebana.

Flowers are always pretty, but with ikebana, you try to put just a few of them together in a way that makes you see their simple beauty. The whole idea is that

less is more!

You're also supposed to be silent while you arrange the flowers, because ikebana is like meditation. It helps you feel peaceful and one with the universe.

Here's what my ikebana looked like today:

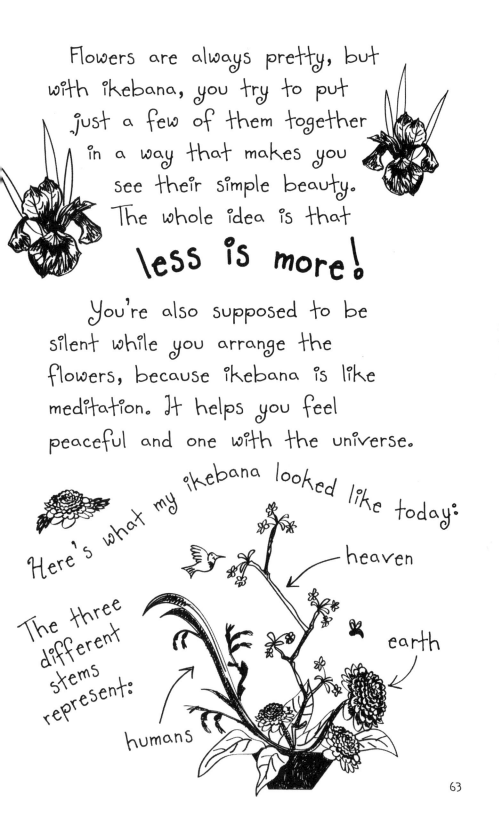

heaven

earth

The three different stems represent:

humans

63

I tried to experience the peace of ikebana today. I really did. But as I trimmed the extra orange curly flowers off their stubby little stalks,

I couldn't stop imagining they were Aldo's head.

My inner monologue* kept saying: He is such an imbecile*!

64

Exhibit A:

How could he not know I'm adopted? ——→

I mean, being adopted isn't who I am—there are so many more essential things about me that make me, me!—but you have to be completely inattentive* to miss the fact that I don't look anything like my red-headed mother, my freckly father, or my blonde sister.

Exhibit B:

And poor Jack! Aldo told him that Hazel might be his new mom?! That is so insensitive*! Jack already has a fantastic mom, for one thing. And Jack is the most important person in the world to his dad! Fritz would never get remarried unless 1] Jack thought it was a good idea, and 2] Fritz knew for sure that his new wife would be a wonderful stepmom to Jack. These things take time! And paying attention to other people's feelings!

All right... I'm now going to calm down by focusing on my ikebana and my breathing.
In, 2, 3, 4, 5. Out, 2, 3, 4, 5.

And now I'm going to draw some much-needed love and acceptance into this sketchbook.

A Note to All Sketchbook Contributors:

Being an imbecile is impolite.

67

INVITATIONS

My mom made me sit down with her to make birthday party invitations after school today.

"Can't we just use Evite?" I pleaded.

"That's too impersonal,*" she said. "Besides, this will be fun."

"You and me...we've got inverse* ideas of fun."

SHE'D ALREADY CUT BROWN PAPER BOWS, LIKE THIS:

NOT THIS KIND OF BOWS:

AND LITTLE BLACK PAPER ARROWS, LIKE THIS:

NEXT WE PASTED THE BOWS TO THE FRONT OF A RED PIECE OF PAPER, LIKE THIS:

THEN WE CUT SLITS IN THE RED PAPER TO THREAD THE ARROW THROUGH, LIKE THIS:

WE ADDED SOME STRING, SOME WORDS, AND ANOTHER PIECE OF PAPER ON THE BACK TO HIDE THE SLITS.

THE FINISHED INVITATION LOOKED LIKE THIS:

Shoot on over to Aldo's 11th Birthday Party!

They were kinda embarrassing, kinda cool. Which could be the title of my autobiography one day.

KINDA EMBARRASSING, KINDA COOL

THE STORY OF MY LIFE
BY ALDO ZELNICK

THE COVER MIGHT LOOK LIKE THIS.

Mom handed me scissors and said, "The good news is the doctor said you could do a little archery for your party, as long as you take it easy."

"Nice," I said. "And I was thinking we could have beef jerky while we shoot, ya know, for a warrior snack."

69

"All right... But the bad news is...you're not inviting Bee?"

"No! Everyone knows you can't have one girl at a boy party! It's like...intermingling* one gummy bear into the bag of beef jerky. It's...incongruous.*"

"Oh pffft. When you were little, all your little girl friends came to your parties."

HELLOOO, CUPCAKES...

ALDO'S ALWAYS BEEN IMMATURE* FOR HIS AGE.

"Mom, I'm not a 1-ounce baby anymore."

"And pretty soon, when you're 13 or 14, you'll want as many girls as possible at your party!"

"Not gonna happen. But also, I'm not 13. I'll only be 11! Sheesh. My own mother can't even remember how old I am..."

"But Bee is your friend!"

I closed my mouth and quietly cut arrows for a couple minutes. I knew I had to come up with a final blow that would defeat Mom-power. Mom-power is infinity times stronger than Hercules.

Finally I thought of something. "You know how there are certain things that you do with just your mom friends?" I said. "Like shopping? Or book club? That's how my birthday party is. It doesn't mean I'm not friends with Bee, it just means it's a guy thing. OK??!!"

My mom scrunched her mouth all the way to one side and looked with her eyes to the other side. It's a face that means, "Hm. You've got a point there."

"Hm. You've got a point there," she said. "OK. Then how about we invite Bee to your family birthday dinner on Sunday?"

"Great! An extra present it is!"

71

About then Dad asked me to go borrow some Italian spices from Mr. Mot for the lasagna he's making. So I trudged all the way over to Mr. Mot's house and knocked on his door...and Goosy answered!

"What are _you_ doing here?" I said.

"Well if isn't my impudent* imp* of a grandson," said Goosy.

"Oh. Sorry. Good evening, grandmother dearest. What are _you_ doing here?"

"Wouldn't you like to know." And she winked at me!

Just then Mr. Mot joined her in the doorway. He handed me a spice jar. "Here's the seasoning your father requested," he said. "How is _The Indian in the Cupboard_ coming along?"

"Good. I liked the part where the kid puts the Indian in his pocket and takes him to school and then the Indian keeps stabbing the kid's leg because he wants to get out..."

72

"Indeed!" Mr. Mot interrupted.* "Goodnight!" And he shut the door. What is it with grown-ups, anyway?

p.s. Here's what the back of the invitations looked like:

- Saturday, February 14th
- 4pm till Sunday morning at 10am
- Aldo's house
- Archery followed by a sleepover

No VALENTINES OR GIRLS ALLOWED. ANY HEARTS OR LACE WILL BE IMMEDIATELY INCINERATED.*

Tomorrow I'm giving these babies to Jack, Danny, Grover, Marvin, Emilio, and Tommy Geller.

p.p.s. Ikebana?! More like ick-ebana!

p.p.p.s. I'm gonna make a sign to tape on our front door during my birthday party. You know, so no interlopers* try to get in.

73

➤ HALT! ◄

PRIVATE BIRTHDAY PARTY IN PROGRESS

ONLY THINGS ON THIS LIST ARE ALLOWED:

ARCHERY

BURPING

CAKE WITH BACON

DEBRIS

ENGAGING IN COMBAT

FLATULENCE

GUYS

HOT WINGS

IRON MAN

JERKY

KARATE

LOUDNESS

MUSCLES

NATURAL SMELLS

OMELETS

PRESENTS

QUIET—NOT!

REBELS

SLEEPING—NOT!

THUMB WARS

UPROAR

VIDEO GAMES

WRESTLING

EXCITEMENT

YOLO

ZOTZ
(THE BEST CANDY EVER!)

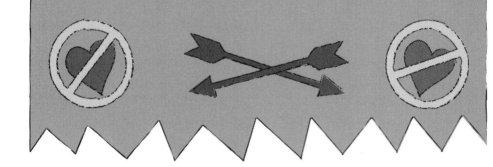

THE BACHELOR

Today at recess I passed out the invitations. Furtively. You know, since I'm not inviting everyone.

THAT'S RIGHT, DANNY. YOU'RE ONE OF THE CHOSEN FEW.

I'M INVITED! YESSS.

Then after school I stopped at the art room to take back some ink I'd borrowed, and guess what I was lucky enough to witness? Ms. Munroe and that hirsute boyfriend of hers, sitting side by

75

side behind her desk, sharing one Icee with two straws. I chucked the ink into its bin and hustled out of there as fast as I could.

WHAT DOES HIRSUTE MEAN AGAIN?

HAIRY. AS IN LOTS OF HAIR. WHICH I LOVE, BY THE WAY.

(New rule: The only time people are allowed to share a beverage in my presence is when they bike to the convenience store with their best friend for Slushies and they're all hot and sweaty and one of them realizes he forgot his money so they have to share because otherwise the impoverished* person would die of thirst. Yes, I know this from experience.)

Then I hurried outside to get home to some History Channel. In the parking lot I spotted Mr. Fodder, the school lunch lady who's a guy.

HEY, MR. FODDER! COOL CAR!

YEAH, IT'S A 1996 CHEVY IMPALA.* FOUR-DOOR. TAPE DECK. A REAL CLASSIC.

"Wow. So anyways, you're a bachelor, right?" I said.

"Yes. Yes, I am."

"That's the way to go, right? You're invincible*! You can do anything you want! I mean, all the superheroes are bachelors, pretty much... Girls just mess things up, like in *Iron Man*..."

"Oh, being single isn't so bad," he said. "But now and again I wish I had someone besides Greta to take for a ride in the Impala..."

77

"Are you doin' anything for Valentine's Day?"

"Well, it <u>is</u> the day I usually iron my spring slacks..."

"You should come to my birthday party! We're gonna do archery and buffalo wings and video games."

"Sounds manlike."

"Oh good. That's what I was going for. I'll have my mom call your mom. Or, I guess my mom will call you."

Good deed for the day, check. Just call me The Most Thoughtful Kid Ever.

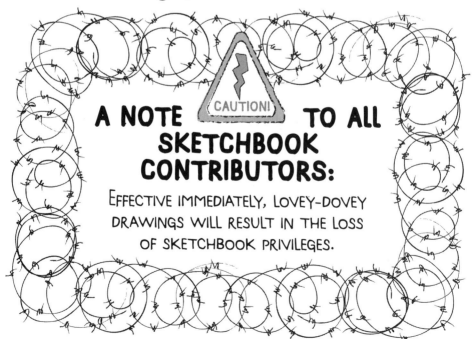

A NOTE CAUTION! **TO ALL SKETCHBOOK CONTRIBUTORS:**
EFFECTIVE IMMEDIATELY, LOVEY-DOVEY DRAWINGS WILL RESULT IN THE LOSS OF SKETCHBOOK PRIVILEGES.

[silver]

[gold]

Make New Friends (and Tolerate the Old)

After school today I got to go to Fare with my mom to help prepare for Valentine's Day dinner. Fare is the restaurant my parents and their friends own.

fare

While my mom made a test batch of roasted-beet bisque, I tore a head of lettuce into bite-sized pieces for a test salad

strawberry slices, toasted walnuts, and bleu cheese crumbles drizzled with strawberry dressing on a bed of crunchy iceberg.

My mom named it the Sweetheart Salad. It's divine!

Oops. that one slipped out!

hola!

$x + y = z$

$2x + 3 - y = \frac{1}{4}$

As I sampled the salad, I sat in a booth and did my algebra homework. My dad teaches me math. He's an engineer. I'm homeschooled, but I go to Dana Elementary for band, Spanish, art, P.E., and, sometimes, lunch and recess. I've made some special friends there, even though one of them, whose initials are A.V.Z., is incorrigible.*

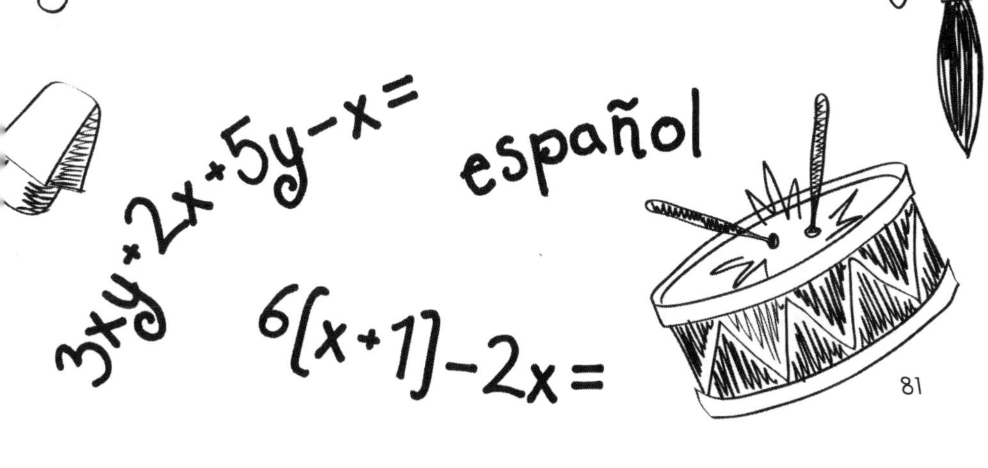

$3xy + 2x + 5y - x =$

español

$6(x + 1) - 2x =$

81

I like having a booth all to myself while the restaurant is empty. I can imagine* I'm in a café somewhere...

somewhere amazing, like Ireland or Istanbul, enjoying a romantic dinner with the boy of my dreams...

"You're all alone!" came a loud voice.

Startled from my daydream, I found a girl standing by my booth. She had long, dark hair in a single braid down past her waist. Her eyes were enormous and black. She placed her delicate hands on my table.

"Well?"

"Oh! No, I'm here with my mom. She's working in the kitchen."

"That's my family," she said, pointing to a table with a mom, a dad, and two other girls. All of them shared the same midnight hair and eyes.

"We're here to eat. But I've never been to this restaurant before. Is it good?"

"By the way... my name is Jyla."

Her voice blared in the quiet restaurant. Her mom gave her a stern look and held a finger to her lips.

Shhh...

"I'm Bee," I said. "And, yes, this restaurant is really good."

"I'm 11. I go to Ibbotson Elementary."

Jyla slid into the seat across from me. Her words came out in intense* bursts that reminded me of Aldo's trumpet.

"Let's play cards."

And from her pocket she produced a pack of playing cards.

While she waited for her meal, Jyla taught me how to play Indian Rummy*! Then after they'd finished eating, her sisters came to my booth too. All three of them look like fairy-tale princesses.

← Jyla

Too soon it was time for them to go.

85

My mom came out from the kitchen and introduced* herself to Jyla's parents. Jyla and I traded phone numbers. Our parents said we could have a play date this weekend!

❀ Tonight I made a new friend! Aldo will be happy to know that she's a girl. I'm happy to know that too. ❀

p.s. I can't make it to a certain person's birthday party on Saturday, anyway, because Jyla and I have plans.

And it's obvious to everyone but Aldo that Mr. Fodder is lonely for romance, not for shooting sports and dried meat.

 # I SPY

Tonight after I finished writing my book report, I went with Jack and his mom to visit Abuelo— that's Jack's grandpa—in the old people home where he lives. I like to keep in touch with Abuelo, since I was the one who saved his life on Halloween night—not like it was a big deal or anything.

We brought a box of Valentine chocolates to his room, then the 4 of us mosied down to the fountain room. That's the giant area where everyone who lives there eats and watches TV. It has a real spraying water fountain in the middle. All over the fountain room's ceiling hung a flock of iridescent* pink paper hearts—decorations for the Valentine's Day dance they're going to have there this Saturday night.

87

"Abuelo loves to dance, don't you, Papá," said Mrs. Lopez. She squeezed his hands in hers.

Abuelo didn't answer. I guess when his memory left, his words left with it.

I looked around at all the old people and wondered how they could dance when it seemed like they could barely walk. That's when I realized that Fountain House is chock-full of <u>grandmas</u>!

THAT ABUELO IS HUNKY.

I'M KNITTING HIM A PINK VALENTINE'S SCARF.

YEP. I'VE STILL GOT IT.

"Hey, what happened to all the grandpas?" I asked.

Jack shrugged. "I think they die first."

"What?" This was news to me! Horrific news! "But Abuelo's still alive!"

"Women don't always live longer than men," said Mrs. Lopez. "But much of the time, that's the way it goes."

"That is so not fair! I wish I was a girl. Wait, what did I just say? What happened to Abuelo's grandma?"

"You mean his wife? My mother? They were married almost 50 years. She passed away more than 10 years ago. We all miss her very much."

"Oh." For the first time ever I had an inkling* about what that "till death do us part" marriage stuff means. So this is what it looks like. I hung my head and pretended to be invisible.*

"Aldo and Jack, as long as you take good care of your bodies, you will live very long, happy lives," added Mrs. Lopez. "Do not worry."

Immediately I began to worry.

"I spy a wig!" cried Jack.

Good ol' Jack. I jumped up and looked around. "There!" I said, pointing to the old lady with bright red hair. It's moments like these when I'm glad my best friend is a subject-changer. We took turns playing I Spy until it was time to leave.

We walked Abuelo back to his room and circled his tiny raisin body in a group hug. Then as we left his room, I turned back to wave at him. There he stood, clutching his still-unopened box of heart chocolates to his chest.

For some reason the Abuelo visit gave me the impetus* to pull out my trumpet and practice "Dancing With Myself" when I got home. It's a weirdly bouncy song for such a glum subject.

90

p.s. Mr. Fodder does <u>so</u> like jerky. I know because I asked him today. And also, he has an archery merit badge from Boy Scouts. So there.

p.p.s. My mom just reminded me that tomorrow is the class Valentine's party. *Gah!* I don't know what to do! Should I write out Valentines for everyone so I can <u>get</u> Valentines (and the candy that comes with them)...or should I skip both?

FRIDAY THE 13TH...

...was a day that lived up to its reputation.

First thing this morning, in band class, Bee demanded the sketchbook.

"It's my turn!" she sang.

"Nope. I clearly stated that lovey-dovey drawings would result in the loss of sketchbook privileges. You drew <u>flowers</u> and <u>hearts</u>."

"Don't be silly. I was just being me!"

"You can fill your own sketchbooks with all the insidious* romance you want. But not <u>my</u> sketchbook. Not anymore."

She crossed her arms across her chest and stomped away. So that went well.

Then this afternoon we had our class Valentine's party. I wore black and camo today, of course, and on my desk I placed a sign that said:

ATTENTION:

I DO NOT OBSERVE VALENTINE'S DAY.

PLEASE DONATE ANY VALENTINES FOR ALDO ZELNICK TO MR. KRUG.

WE APOLOGIZE FOR ANY INCONVENIENCE.*

Kids walked around and handed out their Valentines while I sat at my desk. I have to admit, my intestines* were sad to see all those little bags of M&Ms and Fun-Dips, those precious boxes of Nerds and Milk Duds, those adorable Kit Kats and chocolate kisses, those heart-shaped suckers and peppermint patties, stop for a second at my desk, shrug, then move right on by.

93

When Bee passed out her frilly handmade Valentines, I pretended to be inspecting* the cuffs of my cargo pants. Awkward!

Jack tried to hand me a Wimpy Kid Valentine with a peanut butter cup attached. "At least take this one," he whispered. "These are your favorite."

"I can't, dude."

"Really? Not even from me?"

YOU SEEM INSISTENT,* MR. REESES. HOW 'BOUT I TALK IT OVER WITH MANAGEMENT.

HOW 'BOUT I MAKE YOU AN OFFER YOU CAN'T REFUSE.

NEVER UNDERESTIMATE THE POWER OF PEANUT BUTTER.

ATTENTION:

94

From across the room, I could feel Bee's eyes on me like insects on an open pop can. I shook my head. "Later," I whispered to Jack.

On the walk home from school, Jack showed me his Valentine loot.

"Check out all this candy!" he said.

"Pretty good haul this year."

"I know! And you turned it down! Are you insane?"

Right when Jack was handing me the peanut butter cup, out popped an impediment* named Bee from behind a bush.

"Aha!" she cried. "I thought you weren't observing Valentine's Day, Aldo Valentine!"

"I'm not! I was just going to...throw it away!" And I flung the candy—my favorite candy—into the gutter. "Stop following me!"

"Why would I follow an ignoramus* like you!" she hollered.

Just then, Danny rode by on his bike.

Bee instantaneously* shape-shifted from crazy person to girly-girl. She waved and called, "Hi, Danny! Have a nice Valentine's Day!"

Normally I would have reminded her that Danny couldn't hear her. But instead I just shook my head and kept on walking.

"All the girls think Danny is cute," said Jack as we got to his dad-house. "I wish I was cute."

"Oh c'mon! Cute is a curse," I said. "You saw how Bee acted when she saw Danny. You don't want impressionable* girls going all Disney Channel on you like that! You and me, we're guys' guys. Right?" And I punched him in the arm, cuz that's what guys' guys do.

Then when I finally got home, my mom ambushed me.

"How'd the Valentine's party go?"

"Dandy," I said.

DID YOU GIVE OUT VALENTINES?

No.

DID YOU ACCEPT ANY VALENTINES FROM YOUR CLASSMATES?

No.

SO WHERE'S THE BAG OF MIKE & IKES I GAVE YOU?

IN MY ROOM.

GO GET IT. I WANT IT BACK.

I CAN'T—I.E.,* I ATE THEM.

ALL OF THEM?!

I SAID THE BAG WAS IN MY ROOM. I NEVER SAID THERE WAS ANYTHING IN IT.

97

"Then you owe me 4 dollars for the candy. However, you're in luck! The snow in the back yard melted enough for you to poop-scoop today, which I will accept as payment. Get going, before it gets dark! Oh, and since I forgot to send your class birthday treat to school with you today, you can bring it on Monday. Here, put these in your backpack right now so you don't forget."

Yup, 4 boxes of Little Debbie heart cakes.

"You promised no Valentine's stuff for my birthday!" I said. "When I break the rules, I have to shovel dog poop. But when you break a promise, it's OK?"

"You love Little Debbies!"

"Oh sure! Use my weakness for moist snack cakes against me!"

The day before my birthday was <u>not</u> a great day. Let's hope my birthday is better.

Tools. Fire. Raw meat. Wilderness survival. Body hair. Plaid.

Yup. I'm a dude.

THE MORNING OF

"There's our birthday boy!" said Mom when I shuffled into the kitchen this morning. She trapped me in a hug and planted 11 kisses all over my face.

So as not to cause trouble, I stood still for the assault. But when she was done, I handed her a "I have a severe saliva allergy" card, which I'd placed in my robe pocket just in case.

Meanwhile, Dad was pouring steaming coffee into a mug. "So 11, huh?" he said. "You're probably ready to start drinking coffee now. Do you take cream, or do you want to go with plain black?"

I decided to call his bluff. "Cream," I said. "And a little sugar."

99

Timothy picked up his head from where it was sleeping on the kitchen island just long enough to incoherently* mumble, "Happy birthday, bro." Then he dropped it back down onto his crossed arms and reclosed his eyes.

TIMOTHY'S 15. IS THIS WHAT I HAVE TO LOOK FORWARD TO 4 YEARS FROM NOW? MAYBE HE DOESN'T KNOW ABOUT COFFEE...

While I sipped my delectable coffee (when Dad wasn't looking I poured some of the coffee into the sink so there was room for me to add more cream and more sugar), we had a team meeting about getting ready for my party—which is tonight!

COFFEE 101

1. POUR A CUP ABOUT HALF-FULL WITH COFFEE YOUR PARENTS MADE.

MAXIMUM

2. FILL THE CUP THE REST OF THE WAY WITH CREAM.

3. ADD 3 TO 10 SPOONFULS OF SUGAR AND STIR.

"I'll be cleaning the house while your dad makes your birthday cake," said Mom.

"Oh yeah!" I remembered. "My cake!" My dad loves making big, fancy cakes, and every year I get to choose how my birthday cake will be decorated.

"I was thinking a big red mouth in a smoochy position," said Dad, making kissy fish lips to demonstrate.

"That's real funny. Almost as funny as picking Valentine for your son's middle name," I said. I'd left the Indian in the Cupboard book on the counter and it caught my eye. "I know! How about cowboys and Indians? Like with guns and arrows and tomahawks and red frosting like blood dribbled all over?"

AND THE CAKE BATTER COULD HAVE CHOPPED BACON IN IT. AND HOT SAUCE! WELL, MAYBE NOT HOT SAUCE...

I SCREAM FOR

"Charming," said Mom.

101

"Dude," said Timothy, opening his eyes and raising his head for the second time. "You guys should totally have an Indian wrestling contest tonight."

Mom left the kitchen muttering something about too much testosterone in this house. (Note to self: Tell Mom that her muttering volume needs adjusting too.)

"What's testosterone again?" I asked.

"When a boy becomes a man...," Timothy started to say.

Dad interrupted him. "It's basically guy power."

"Welp," I said, "there's no such thing as too much guy power! Am I right or am I right?"

Dad and Timothy high-fived me their agreement, while Max, the fourth boy in the room, wagged and let out a long, slow toot.

As the owner of the most sensitive Zelnick family nose, I can confirm that this house now SMELLS like guy power too.

I'm supposed to be making my room immaculate*
right now, but instead I'm chillaxing in my fort-
closet, working on my sketchbook. It's <u>my</u> birthday,
after all. Wait a sec. I hear Dad calling my name.

Dad snuck into my room with a big black
trash bag chock-full of toy bows and arrows!

COLOR-CODED AND EVERYTHING!

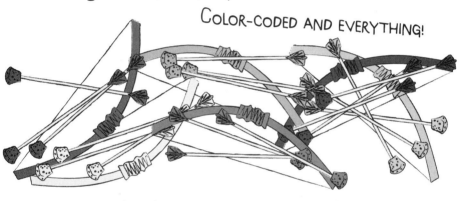

"I bought these for you and your buddies
to play with at our house tonight," he whispered.
"The arrows are tipped with foam, so nobody will
get hurt. But man, do they ever fly!"

He fitted an arrow to the bow, pulled back
the string, and released the arrow. It whizzed
across my bedroom and bonked straight into
Bogus's glass bowl. The water wobbled, but bowl
and fish remained intact.*

103

FISH AREN'T EASILY IRRITATED,* BUT MOST FISH DON'T HAVE TO LIVE WITH ALDO ZELNICK.

"Sweet," I said. "Thanks, Dad!"

"I don't think we should tell Mom about this quite yet, though," he continued in murmur volume. "But she'll be fine with it once she gets into the party spirit."

So everything's falling into place for the Best. Birthday. Party. Ever. We've got weapons. Manly cake. Dad's also making hot wings and homemade pepperoni pizza rolls. Plenty of Coke. Boys-only. And not one Valentine in sight.

Happy birthday to me!

THE MORNING AFTER

Have you ever been so tired that you can't sleep? That's me right now. So I might as well get everything down on sketchbook paper, while the shocking details are still fresh.

My birthday party started nice and usual, at 4 in the afternoon, when an influx* of birthday party invitees* arrived at my house just like clockwork: Jack, Danny, Grover, Marvin, Emilio, Tommy Geller, and Mr. Fodder.

One by one they came to my front door, where I'd posted the list of things that were allowed to enter—the list that made all the moms laugh when they dropped off their boys.

105

Each kid carried a birthday present (yesss), a sleeping bag, and a backpack  with overnight stuff their moms <u>made</u> them bring, such as a toothbrush (like that was ever gonna get used), and stuff they <u>wanted</u> to bring, like their iPods. They piled the presents on the dining room table, then Mom had them stow their gear in my bedroom and climb into our minivan so we could drive to the archery place. (We couldn't all fit, so Mr. Fodder drove himself, Timothy, and my dad in the Impala.)

The archery guy set us up with bows and arrows and gave us the safety lesson. You know... no pointing arrows at other people. No walking toward the target to pick up shot arrows until he blew the whistle. Etcetera.

He taught us what all the bow and arrow parts and pieces are called and how to stand correctly. I thought there was more or less only 1 way to stand, but it turns out that there's standing, then there's "getting into a stance."

106

REGULAR STANDING

Archery stance means standing sideways, making your back straight like the spine of a book, sucking in your belly, then pulling back like Hercules on the bowstring.

Standing this way takes neck muscles, back muscles, stomach muscles, and arm muscles. Which is a lot of muscles. Good thing mine are getting pretty developed these days.

ARCHERY STANCE

107

There were 3 paper targets taped onto big foam pads, so 3 of us could shoot at the same time. The archery guy said the birthday boy always shoots the first arrow. So with everyone's eyes on me, I nocked an arrow, pulled back, and let go. Not only did it miss my target, it shot straight into the ceiling and stuck there. It wiggled for a couple seconds, just to insult* me.

"He-he. Just wanted to make it OK for everyone to mess up!" I called out. "Whose idea was it to do archery again?" I whispered to Jack.

"Yours," he reminded me.

We each got to shoot a quiver of 10 arrows, twice. (A quiver—that's what us archers call the arrow-holder tube.) One of my arrows even hit the target!

THIS IS WHAT THE ARCHERY RANGE LOOKS LIKE INSIDE.

MY 10 ARROWS BEFORE

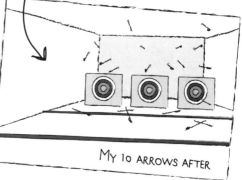

MY 10 ARROWS AFTER

108

Of course, Timothy won the green Robin Hood hat my mom brought as a prize for the most bullseyes, but for some reason Mr. Fodder thought she said his name and rushed forward to claim it. He snatched it from her hands then gave such a deep bow and impressive* wave of his new hat before setting it on his big ol' head that nobody pointed out his mistake.

AND THAT'S HOW IT'S DONE, BOYS.

Post-archery, we all came back to my house to try to satisfy our insatiable* hunger for pizza rolls and hot wings.

Then we were thirsty from all the activity and salt, so we drank a bunch of Coke.

Which created the ideal* conditions for...you guessed it, a burping contest.

Marvin burped the longest burp—7 seconds.

Danny burped the loudest, which was ironic,* since he couldn't even hear it. He sign-languaged that he could _feel_ its loudness though.

Mr. Fodder taught us to talk-burp. That's where you say words while you're burping. Everybody said-burped, "Happy Birthday, Aldo." It was exquisite.

After the belchfest we moved on to video games. But one of the imperfections* of video games (maybe the only imperfection, actually) is that unless you're Grover and have a giant video game room wall-to-wall with consoles and controllers, it's hard to play them with a bunch of people.

110

So we quit the video games and moved on to Indian wrestling, just like Timothy suggested. In case you don't know how to Indian wrestle, it's easy. Two kids just lie down (facing up) next to each other on the floor, with their heads at opposite ends. Then each of you raises the leg that's closest to the other person, and you hook your two legs together at the knee. Then you try to pull your own knee back down to the ground, which basically makes the other kid flip over. Whoever flips loses.

RED ROVER, RED ROVER, I'LL MAKE GROVER ROLL OVER!

YOU'RE GOING DOWN IN IGNOMINIOUS* DEFEAT, GELLER!

JUST THINK OF IT AS ARM WRESTLING, ONLY WITH LEGS. IT'S ONE OF THE FEW SPORTS WHERE YOU LOOK UP AT THE SKY WHILE YOU DO IT. DON'T ASK ME WHY IT'S CALLED INDIAN WRESTLING THOUGH.

111

Now, you know me—I'm usually pretty iffy*

about activities that involve perspiration, but we

wrestled till we were sweaty like spaghetti—and it

was good. Tommy Geller's face got so red and drippy

he looked like a cherry popsicle on the 4th of July.

Then we dripped our way to the kitchen,

because Mom called us to cake and ice cream.

Check out how the cake Dad made looked before

we devoured it:

THE TEEPEE IS AN OLD PARTY HAT COVERED IN A BROWN PAPER BAG!

CHECK OUT THE 12-CANDLE CAMPFIRE—WITH TOOTSIE ROLL LOGS AND A FIRE PIT MADE OUT OF CHOCOLATE ROCKS!

MOST OF THESE ARE LITTLE PLASTIC COWBOYS... BUT A FEW ARMY MEN SNUCK IN.

112

Everybody sang "Happy Birthday, Dear Aldo," I blew out my 12 candles (11 plus 1 to grow on, my mom says) and made a wish, and then I got to open presents! To tell you the truth, I'd been so intent* on planning a guy party for the last couple of weeks that I'd barely thought about presents! And that's just not like me.

I got a boomerang and a catapult kit and a plastic lightsaber with sound effects. Grover gave me a wallet that he made himself out of bacon-patterned duct tape. Inside the wallet was a gift card to GameStop. Bonus!

Jack gave me a rock hammer. "You never know when you might need a rock hammer," he said.

"I was just thinking the same thing," I said. "Um, thanks."

"Time for the bows and arrows?" whispered Dad.

"Indubitably*!" It was totally time for the bows and arrows.

113

WE INTERRUPT THIS PARTY...

Let's pause to enjoy the perfection that was, up until that moment, Aldo Valentine Zelnick's 11th birthday.

Because if right about now you're thinking that it was pretty much the greatest guy party in the history of testosterone, you'd be right. There were was so much guy power under our roof, it could've intimidated* Marines. It would've made Iron Man look infantile.* It should've won us a Guinness World Record for birthday boyness.

Plus, no pink. No dancing. No girls (except my mom, who is a mom). And not a single Valentine! In fact, for the first time in my birthday life, I'd completely forgotten that it was Valentine's Day.

Unpause. *Sigh.*

I ran up to my fort-closet, where Dad had left the trash bag full of toy bows and arrows.

This sketchbook was sitting, open, on the floor next to the trash bag. That is not where I'd left it. Weird. I grabbed the trash bag and carried it out to the boy herd.

20 arms reached in and grabbed bows and arrows. 10 arrows zoomed every which way. Then 10 more. Then there were legs in jeans running all over the house and there was whooping and grabbing up arrows off the floor and jumping off chairs and falling with pretend injuries and generally letting go of any civilized inhibitions* we might have still had.

115

"Holy smokes," I heard Dad say.

I grabbed a sleeping bag, unrolled it, and, still standing, zipped myself inside it. It would be good protection, I thought. Like body armor, only comfortable.

So there I was, standing inside the sleeping bag. I was just inside the front door shooting an arrow at Emilio, who was sliding down the stair railing and shooting an arrow at me at the same time, when I heard the doorbell ring.

I opened the door. There stood Goosy and Mr. Mot and Mrs. Dulcet.

Goosy swooped in to hug and smooch me. "Happy birthday, my Valentine!" she said. "We've come to see how your party is going."

"Yeaaahhh...," I said. "We're kinda in the middle of a war here."

"Oh this'll just take a minute." And in they came.

Goosy loud-whistled, which got everyone's attention. "Happy Aldo's birthday!" she called. "We've just been to Fountain House, which is the old folks' home where Jack's Abuelo lives. They had a Valentine's Day dance there tonight. So for the past few weeks, the three of us—Mr. Mot, Mrs. Dulcet, and I—have been teaching ourselves how to do the Cupid Shuffle so we could show the Fountain House residents. And now we're here to share the love with you fellas too."

She popped her iPod into our speaker. It started playing a rap song. And before I could throw a fit, there was dancing and cupid-song singing at my birthday party.

THE CUPID SHUFFLE:

TO THE RIGHT	TO THE LEFT	NOW KICK	NOW WALK IT BY YOURSELF
TO THE RIGHT	TO THE LEFT	NOW KICK	
TO THE RIGHT	TO THE LEFT	NOW KICK	WALK, WALK IT BY
TO THE RIGHT	TO THE LEFT	NOW KICK	YOURSELF

Jack was dancing. Timothy was dancing. Danny was dancing. Actually, all the kids were dancing. And my mom and dad were dancing. Even Mr. Fodder was dancing. But I was not dancing. Even though it looked medium fun, it was not on the list of allowed things!

At least there aren't any girls, I thought. Moms and grandmas, but not real girls.

And that's when I saw Bee. She was dancing too. And there was another girl dancing next to her! A girl with long, black hair and eyes like giant watermelon seeds, but in a nice way.

118

"Hey!" I shouted, poking Bee in the shoulder. "What are you doing here?"

WE WANT TO BE WARRIORS, JUST LIKE YOU GUYS!

"We crashed your party!" she yelled over the music. "We're rebels, just like it says on the list on the front door! This is my new friend, Iyla!"

"How'd you get in?"

"We knocked and your mom let us in while you were opening presents!"

"You're not invited! Nothing personal, Iyla."

"Well we're here!" she replied indifferently.*

I wasn't just mad. I was irate.* But it was so loud and wild in the room that I couldn't concentrate on what to do about it. And I was still sausaged inside the sleeping bag. But I did have a bow and arrow! So I nocked a foam arrow and pointed it across the room, at the iPod speaker. *If I can just stop the music,* I was thinking, *then I can regain guy control of this party. Goosy and Mr. Mot and Mrs. Dulcet will go home and Bee and her friend will leave too.*

119

But right then, Bee stuck her tongue out at me. I swear! Before my brain realized what my arms were doing, I shot the arrow at her instead.

In my defense, I'd like to remind you that all of us boys had just been having an epic bow-and-arrow battle. We'd been shooting the foam arrows at each other with impunity,* and it was fun. Fun, I tell you!

But Bee...she did not think that taking an arrow to the face was fun. It knocked her glasses to the floor, where they were immediately Cupid Shuffled on by Mr. Fodder. Who is not a small human.

That's when the song ended. The dancing stopped. The room got much quieter, as everyone caught their breath. Danny picked up Bee's cracked glasses and handed them to her.

120

Yeah, when I replay the scene in my brain, I can see that this wasn't the ideal time for me to be indiscreet.* But right then, I was too infuriated* to see it. So I shrieked. At Bee. Loud enough that everyone in the whole neighborhood probably heard. Everyone except for Danny, but he can lip read, so...

JUST BECAUSE YOU'RE IN LOVE WITH DANNY PETERSON, BEE, DOES NOT MAKE IT OK FOR YOU TO INVITE YOURSELF TO MY BIRTHDAY PARTY!

And Bee started to cry.

I'd never seen her cry before. Ever. Not even that one time when we were bike riding and I kinda sorta accidentally cut in front of her and she fell and practically impaled herself on a rose bush.

121

Bee ran out the front door. I ran out after her. I wanted to catch up to her, but Bee runs a lot faster than I do. She disappeared into the darkness.

Next Lyla came busting out the door. "I'LL TALK TO BEE," she blurted as she ran past me. "SHE'S MY FRIEND."

Her voice surprised me. It didn't sound pretty, like her eyes. Actually, it sounded kinda goatish. But that didn't matter, because it was the meaning of the words that really stuck me like an arrow to the heart: She was Bee's friend.

I went back inside, only to find everyone standing there, dead quiet, with their arms crossed over their chests. They all glared icily* at me.

"What?!" I said. "She's the one who wrecked my party! My perfect party!" I said it, but I knew it wasn't true.

And I stomped upstairs, burst into my fort-closet, slammed the door, and sprawled on the floor in the dark. Which is where I've been, all by myself, ever since.

122

Mom came once and said through the door, "I'm sorry I let Bee and her friend in, because you and I had agreed it was a guy party. But you need to apologize to her."

"Go away," I said.

Jack came once and said through the door, "We're all watching the *Iron Mans* in the living room until we fall asleep. You should come."

"Go away," I said.

Mr. Fodder came once and said through the door, "I'm leaving now, Aldo. Thanks for inviting me."

"You're welcome. I'm really glad you came," I said. "Now go away."

Dad came once and said through the door, "Guess I caused some problems with those bows and arrows, huh, sport. I brought you some popcorn."

123

"Go away," I said. "But first, gimme that popcorn. I'm famished." And I cracked open the door just enough for him to pass me the bag.

I haven't been able to fall asleep, but that's given me time to think about things. And turn on the closet light to write in my sketchbook. And think some more.

Now I know what I need to do. Which, the first thing is, get a drink! Never eat popcorn while locked up in a closet without a beverage! Then I'm gonna get busy, before everyone else wakes up. It's super early in the morning on February 15th, a new day.

Sometimes aren't you just so relieved there's such a thing as new days?

124

Ignoramus

I sprinted home. My mom and dad were in the kitchen, waiting for me and Jyla to return from Aldo's.

"What happened?" they said when they saw my wet cheeks and broken glasses. They rushed over to fold me in a hug.

Before I could answer, Jyla came running into the kitchen and explained everything that had happened at the party.

...And first we hid in the bushes and spied with the binoculars. But then I had to use the bathroom, so Bee knocked on the door...

Everything tastes better in a fancy cup!

Mom and Dad helped us calm down.
They made us hot cocoa.
They brought me my extra pair of glasses.
Then they tucked us into my bed and
kissed us both goodnight.

Jyla and I talked
and talked in the darkness.
I think we were loud, because
Jyla seems incapable* of using
an inside voice,* but my parents
didn't come tell us to quiet down.
They let us giggle and tell
secrets until all the secrets
were free.

With Ping and Pong (they're my cats) snuggled up against us, we compared favorite singers and books and sports and animals. Jyla told me all about her family and what it's like to have 2 sisters instead of just 1. I told her about being adopted and what it's like to have boys for best friends, even though they don't always include me.

"Well... I'll **always** include **you**," she said.

We looked out the window at the stars and talked about what we wanted to be when we grow up. Jyla said she's considering either doctor or librarian. I told her she'd make a wonderful doctor.

"Every day I think of something new to be!" I said. "Like right now, I'm thinking how incredible it would be to be an astronaut!"

"OK," she said. "Let's be doctor astronauts."

I told her about Danny and how I have this flustery feeling about him, like there's a butterfly living in the cage of my ribs.

"I hope the butterfly flies away, though," I said. "It's annoying. And also, I'm not in love with him. That's dumb. I'm not old enough to be in love."

"It's infatuation,*" said Jyla. "You're in like with him. I'm in like with a boy at my school. His name is Ivan. Ivan and Jyla. Sounds great, doesn't it? Too bad he eats boogers."

We must have finally fallen asleep because the next thing I knew, my mom was kissing me awake.

"It's early, but someone's here to see you." She whispered, because Jyla was still sleeping.

I stood and she wrapped my robe around me. I padded down the hall to the kitchen. It was a sunny Sunday, and the glittery Valentines I'd made ceiling sparkled in the morning light. and hung from the

At the kitchen table sat Aldo. He was holding a full cup of coffee, but he looked like a crumpled little boy. I slid into a chair across from him.

I'm sorry your glasses got busted

he said.

I didn't mean to knock them off. It's just that... well, you picked kind of a bad time to stick out your tongue out at me.

I did _not_ stick my tongue out at you! I was concentrating on the Cupid Shuffle moves, that's all. Sometimes my tongue sticks out an itty-bit* when I concentrate,

I said.

Oh. Right. I guess mine sometimes does that too,

he admitted.

130

He reached into his jacket pocket and pulled out a piece of pink construction paper that was as crumpled as his face. He handed it to me. (I decided to tear it in half so I could tape it here and save it forever!)

I'M NOT GOOD AT FLOWERY FEELINGS...

...BUT WE'RE FRIENDS, AND FRIENDS GIVE EACH OTHER VALENTINES FOR SOME REASON.

So HAPPY VALENTINE'S DAY. AND ALSO, NEXT YEAR I HOPE YOU'LL COME TO MY BIRTHDAY PARTY. BRING YOUR IDIOSYNCRATIC* FRIEND IYLA TOO.

YOUR BFF (BOY FRIEND FOREVER, BUT NOT BOYFRIEND),

Aldo Zelnick

A.K.A. IGNORAMUS

"This is nice," I said. I noticed he wasn't drinking his coffee, so I poured him a glass of orange juice. "And I'm sorry I crashed your party. I just really wanted to be there."

132

"You were reading the sketchbook in the fort-closet last night before I realized you were in my house, weren't you," he said. "I found it open on the floor."

"Yes. I was. I wanted to see how it's coming along. Since I'm a contributor and all."

Then he reached into his other jacket pocket and handed me the sketchbook. "Actually, you're the co-author/illustrator, so you should do some more pages. It's getting close to the end."

"Thanks," I said. "But you are still an ignoramus."

"I know. I think it's a guy thing. And you're still a girl. Hey, do you have any leftover pizza from your restaurant?"

I went to the refrigerator and found a few slices of broccoli with bacon. I put them on a plate and microwaved them until they were bubbly, then I carried the plate to the table.

"If I have to **eat crow**, I'm glad it's pizza flavor," he said.

And so, while the rest of the house slept, Aldo Valentine Zelnick and I had breakfast together. He told me all about his birthday party, and I told him all about Jyla and how elated I feel to have a friend who's a she.

"Because you and Jack and the rest of the lost boys are my best friends, but I get kind of tired of being the only Wendy," I said.

"What?" he said.

"Oh never mind."

As he was leaving, Aldo reached into his pocket for a third time. "I almost forgot," he said. "I wanted to give you one more thing." And he handed me a duct-tape wallet with bacon on it.

This Valentine's Day, give the gift of bacon!

"Wow," I said. "Thank you." And I meant it. Aldo adores bacon. So if he gives you something bacon-y, even if it is regifted, you know he must really care about you.

135

BETTER LATE THAN NEVER

Tonight was my family birthday dinner. It's a Zelnick tradition. It's where my dad cooks whatever the birthday person wants, and afterward, the birthday person opens presents from the family. Besides Goosy and Timothy and my parents, Mr. Mot and Bee came too.

While I snarfed down the best chicken enchiladas known to man, Goosy and Mr. Mot told stories about Fountain House and the Cupid Shuffle.

"We showed those most senior of citizens how the younger generation busts a move!" said Mr. Mot.

"You should have seen Mrs. Dulcet!" said Goosy. "She's an impeccable* dancer. So is Abuelo! They waltzed beautifully together."

"Oh I'm so glad!" said Bee. "She had someone to dance with besides herself after all!"

"Her husband passed away several years ago," explained Mr. Mot. "But this year she vowed not to isolate* herself on Valentine's Day. And thus was born her idea for the Fountain House Frolic!"

Oh great, I thought. Mr. Dulcet—another dead dude. At least I'm only 11...

"You're awfully quiet," said Goosy to me as she second-helpinged my plate.

"I didn't sleep so good last night," I muttered.

WHY? IS YOUR IMPROPER GRAMMAR KEEPING YOU UP?

WHATEVER. IT'S MY PARTY AND I CAN USE ADJECTIVES INSTEAD OF ADVERBS IF I WANT TO.

137

"He stayed up to make me a Valentine!" interjected* Bee.

"You did?!" happy-whined Mom. "Awww...that's so sweet!"

"Awww...didja make me one too?" imitated* Timothy.

"Actually," I admitted, sitting up straight and claiming my unique specialness as the February 14th kid, "I stayed up and made all of you Valentines."

And I jumped from my chair to get the sack of *Iron Man* Valentines I'd written out to all the importantest people in my life so far.

I walked around the table, and as I handed each person a better-late-than-never Valentine, I gave him or her a hug too. Except for Timothy. Him I just shoved a little.

When I got to Bee, I gave her a Valentine and leaned in to whisper, "That one's for Iyla."

Unfortunately, Bee does not seem to understand the concept of insider information.* "You made Iyla a Valentine?" she squealed.

138

KEEP EATING, EVERYONE! BEE WAS JUST TALKING WITH HER MOUTH FULL OF FOOD. DISGUSTING! DON'T WORRY, THOUGH. I'M ON IT!

"Uh...at my party I mighta seemed not as cool as I really am," I said. "I didn't want her to have the wrong impression* about me."

"She's a lovely girl," said Dad, winking at me. "She's Indian, right?"

"Well, she lives here," said Bee, "so she's Indian American."

"Wait a sec. Indian?" I said. "She's not the same as the Indian in that book I borrowed from Mr. Mot..."

"That young warrior was not an Indian American but rather an American Indian, of the Iroquois tribe," said Mr. Mot. "They and other Native Americans inhabited* North America for centuries before your ancestors did, Aldo. Young lyla's family, on the other hand, hails from the country of India, on the continent of Asia, on the other side of the globe."

139

Sheesh. I wish all the Indian people wouldn't pick such confusing names. "Can I open presents now?" I said.

I didn't get a laptop computer, but I did get an archery set with real feathers and points on the arrows! (After I opened it, Mom grabbed it. She's keeping it "somewhere safe" until we can go to the archery place again.) Timothy forgot to get me a present, so he gave me an I.O.U.* Bee gave me stick-on moustaches and a kit for cleaning my trumpet. From Mr. Mot I got a booklight. And from Goosy? A pair of footie pajamas with hearts and cupids all over them. *Blerg.*

I gotta put down this sketchbook and go get some sleep. Tomorrow's a school day, and I have heart cakes to pass out.

I KNOW! LET'S GIVE KIDS A DAY OFF FROM SCHOOL.

YOU'RE JUST MAD CUZ I GOT MORE VALENTINES THAN YOU DID.

GEORGE AND MARTHA, SITTIN' IN A TREE... K-I-S-S-I-N-G!

PRESIDENTS' DAY

Welp, a week's gone by and everything's more or less back to usual. Valentine's Day and my 11th birthday already seem like forever ago.

But today is Monday, February 23rd, and you know what that means...no school! Woot-woot! Do we live in a great country or what?

I think I'll text Jack and see if he wants to redo that *Iron Man* marathon I missed at my birthday party. Oh yeah, and I promised Bee I'd stop by her house for a drum lesson. *Blerg.* But first I've gotta finish up this sketchbook and scratch the comic strip itch* I've been feeling.

141

BACON BOY IN

I cannot tell a lie.

THIS TREE IS GETTING ON MY NERVES, C.W..

ZWAKKK!

NO ONE REALLY EVEN LIKES BROCCOLI EXCEPT...

...YOUR FATHER. OH DEAR.

ACK! MY CHERISHED TREE LIES SLAIN UPON THE GROUND!

WHAT HAPPENED, BACON BOY?

I CANNOT TELL A LIE, FATHER... C.W. WAS HUNGRY, AND HE CHEWED RIGHT THROUGH IT.

WHAT IS WRONG WITH YOU???

THE TRUTH IS WORTH A MILLION BROCCOLI TREES. BY THE WAY, WHAT HAPPENED TO THAT HATCHET I GAVE YOU FOR YOUR BIRTHDAY?

GAH! NOW THEY'RE GOING TO START FEEDING ME BROCCOLI! AND WHO GIVES A KID A HATCHET, ANYWAY???!!!

"I" GALLERY

Mr. Mot used to be an English teacher. He's a word nerd, and he likes to help me use awesome words in my sketchbooks. I mark the best words with one of these: * (it's called an asterisk). When you see an * you'll know you can look here, in the Gallery, to see what the word means. If you don't know how to say some of the words, just ask Mr. Mot. Or someone you know who's like Mr. Mot. Or go to aldozelnick.com, and we'll say them for you.

i.e. (pg. 97): in other words...

I.O.U. (pg. 140): I owe you. Get it?

iceberg lettuce (pg. 20): a crunchy, pale green lettuce

icily (pg. 122): with frosty anger

ideal (pg. 109): perfectly perfect

idioms (pg. 32): sayings that mean something other than what the words literally say

idiosyncratic (pg. 132): weirdly unique

idiotic (pg. 51): like a dumb person

idolize (pg. 31): when you're infatuated with a person you think is perfect

iffy (pg. 112): not sure about something—and maybe leaning towards nah

ignominious (pg. 111): shameful

ignoramus (pg. 96): someone who's being really dumb but doesn't know it

ignoring (pg. 27): acting like something doesn't exist

Iliad (pg. 26): a book-long poem about war written by an ancient Greek guy named Homer (not Simpson)

ilk (pg. 28): kind; type

illustrator (pg. 49): someone awesome who draws awesome pictures (like me!) (AND ME!)

imagine (pg. 82): dream up in your brain

imbecile (pg. 64): ignoramus

imitated (pg. 138): mimicked

immaculate (pg. 103): 100% clean and tidy

immature (pg. 70): not all the way grown yet

immortal (pg. 7): never dying

imp (pg. 72): a smallish creature full of playful naughtiness

Impala (pg. 77): a kind of car and also a kind of African antelope

I WAS HERE FIRST.

145

impale (pg. 55): poke something through with a sharp object

impeccable (pg. 136): perfect

impediment (pg. 95): something in the way

MOST FOOD TASTES BETTER IMPALED ON A TOOTHPICK

imperfections (pg. 110): little flaws that make something that is almost perfect, not perfect

impersonal (pg. 68): basic and not caring about the specialness of people

impervious (pg. 60): so strong it blocks stuff. Like, Iron Man's suit is impervious to lasers, and teachers are impervious to kid excuses.

impetus (pg. 90): something that causes something else to happen

impolite (pg. 61): not nice

impoverished (pg. 76): poor

impression (pg. 139): a quick judgment

impressionable (pg. 96): easy to influence

impressive (pg. 109): better than usual

impudent (pg. 72): boldly naughty

impunity (pg. 120): without anything bad happening

in-thing (pg. 23): what the cool people do

inattentive (pg. 65): not paying attention

146

incapable [pg. 126]: can't do something

incinerated (pg. 73): burned

incognito (pg. 160): dressed to look like someone else

incoherently (pg. 100): not clearly or understandably

inconceivable (pg. 42): so weirdly not expected that your brain practically explodes when it happens

incongruous (pg. 70): two things that don't go together...like peanut butter and ketchup

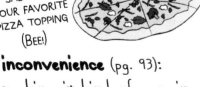

OR LIKE CHOOSING SALAD AS YOUR FAVORITE PIZZA TOPPING (BEE!)

inconvenience (pg. 93): making it kind of a pain to do something

incorrigible [pg. 81]: so irksome that you know the person will never learn to be kind and good all the time

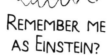

REMEMBER ME AS EINSTEIN?

increased (pg. 34): got bigger and bigger

incredible (pg. 19): way awesome

indefatigable (pg. 53): never tiring out

Indian Rummy [pg. 85]: Such a fun card game!

MEH.

indifferently (pg. 119): like you don't care one way or the other

indiscreet (pg. 121): being loud and showy about something that is a secret

147

indubitably (pg. 113): of course!

inertia (pg. 17): that lazy feeling you get when sitting around and not moving just makes you want to sit around and not move even more

inevitable (pg. 52): something that's going to happen no matter what

infamy (pg. 11): famous because it's so horrible

infantile (pg. 114): babyish

infatuation [pg. 129]: a sweet, innocent kind of love. Love Light.

infected (pg. 12): when something bad gets into something good

inferno (pg. 40): a big fire

infiltrated (pg. 16): snuck in

infinite (pg. 11): forever and ever and ever...ad nauseum

influence (pg. 59): when you change someone's thoughts

influx (pg. 105): a bunch coming at the same time

infringe (pg. 35): crossing the line into territory you're not supposed to go into

infuriated (pg. 121): so mad you're full of fury

ingratiate (pg. 59): do things in a way that makes other people like you

inhabited (pg. 139): lived in

inherent (pg. 43): part of something from the very beginning

inherited (pg. 50): got from your relatives

inhibitions (pg. 115): feelings of shyness that keep you from doing dumb or embarrassing things

inkling (pg. 89): an itty-bit of understanding

inner monologue [pg. 64]: what you think to yourself inside your brain

innocent (pg. 58): not yet understanding the ways of the world

innocuous (pg. 17): harmless

innuendo (pg. 19): a hint that you mean something sneaky

insanely (pg. 32): way outside what most people consider normal

DAD

ALDO

IN THE CASE OF MY GOOD LOOKS, I IN-**HAIR**-ITED THEM.

insatiable (pg. 109): can't be satisfied

inscription (pg. 7): what someone writes in the first couple of pages of a book they gave you as a gift

insensitive [pg. 66]: rude

inside voice [pg. 126]: voice volume anywhere from sigh to talk

insider information (pg. 138): something secret-ish you're not supposed to go blabbing to everyone else

insidious (pg. 92): when something is really good at sneaking its way in

insistent (pg. 94): trying hard to make something happen

inspecting (pg. 94): examining something

instantaneously (pg. 96): right this very second

149

insult (pg. 108): say or do something that's not nice to someone else

intact (pg. 103): whole and unbroken

intelligence (pg. 20): info you get by spying

intense (pg. 84): extreme

intent (pg. 113): focused on

interjected (pg. 138): said in the middle of something

interlopers (pg. 73): people who enter even though they're not supposed to

intermingling (pg. 70): two things that aren't like each other getting all mixed up together

interrogated (pg. 14): questioned

interrupted (pg. 73): This is when (bite, chew, chew, swallow) you're

stopped in the middle of something. I was stopped in the middle of this definition by a piece of beef jerky.

intestines (pg. 93): the long, hose-y squiggles that connect your stomach to your outside

intimidated (pg. 114): made kinda afraid by someone who's more powerful

intolerable (pg. 38): can't be stood

intrepid (pg. 27): brave

introduced (pg. 86): "Reader, meet Jyla. Jyla, meet reader." There. I just introduced you to Jyla. (It's pronounced EYE-la, by the way.)

inventive (pg. 10): good at coming up with new ideas

150

inverse (pg. 68): opposite

invigorating (pg. 49): giving you energy and liveliness

invincible (pg. 77): can't be beaten

invisible (pg. 89):

(Ha! I drew this definition with invisible ink.)

invitees (pg. 105): the people you invite with invitations

iota (pg. 59): the smallest tiny bit you can see with the human eye

irate (pg. 119): so, so mad!!!

iridescent (pg. 87): shiny and rainbowy

irksome (pg. 23): irritating

ironclad (pg. 60): unbreakably strong

ironic (pg. 110): Mr. Mot says irony is a complex rhetorical device...blah, blah, blah. I think it just means that something's funny because two incongruous things are put together or things turn out exactly the opposite of what you expect.

irrationally (pg. 55): in a way that doesn't make logical sense

irritated (pg. 104): annoyed; irked

isolate (pg. 137): leave alone

itch (pg. 141): something you want to do

itinerary (pg. 21): schedule

itty-bit (pg. 130): a little tiny amount

151

MY NEIGHBORHOOD

To Fare (my family's restaurant) and Iris flower shop!

Bee's house!

BIRTHDAY PARTY HQ

MR. MOT'S LIBRARY

To FOUNTAIN HOUSE

TO ICE FISHING LAKE

DANA ELEMENTARY

SLUSHIE STOP

JACK'S DAD-HOUSE

TIMOTHY'S GIRLFRIEND'S HOUSE (AND SITE OF THE TWIZZLER INCIDENT)

TO THE ARCHERY PLACE

award-winning
ABOUT THE ALDO ZELNICK
COMIC NOVEL SERIES

The Aldo Zelnick comic novels are an alphabetical series for middle-grade readers aged 7-13. Rabid and reluctant readers alike enjoy the intelligent humor and drawings as well as the action-packed stories. They've been called vitamin-fortified *Wimpy Kids*.

NOW AVAILABLE!

160 pages | Hardcover
ISBN: 978-1-934649-04-6
$12.95

Part comic romps, part mysteries, and part sesquipedalian-fests (ask Mr. Mot), they're beloved by parents, teachers, and librarians as much as kids.

Artsy-Fartsy introduces ten-year-old Aldo, the star and narrator of the entire series, who lives with his family in Colorado. He's not athletic like his older brother, he's not a rock hound like his best friend, but he does like bacon. And when his artist grandmother, Goosy, gives him a sketchbook to "record all his artsy-fartsy ideas" during summer vacation, it turns out Aldo is a pretty good cartoonist.

In addition to an engaging cartoon story, each book in the series includes an illustrated glossary of fun and challenging words used throughout the book, such as *absurd, abominable,* and *audacious* in *Artsy-Fartsy* and *brazen, behemoth,* and *boisterous* in *Bogus.*

BAILIWICK PRESS

www.bailiwickpress.com | www.aldozelnick.com

ALSO IN THE ALDO ZELNICK COMIC NOVEL SERIES

ACKNOWLEDGMENTS

"To be ignorant of one's ignorance is the malady of the ignorant."
— Amos Bronson Alcott

Aldo is indubitably ignorant of his own ignorance until it's rather dramatically revealed to him. Like many of us, he's a slow and intransigent learner. But say what you will about our now 11-year-old hero, he earns his insights.

One of the insights we've earned in working on this series is that children respond to stories written for and about them—yet the world of children's literature is chockablock with books that were actually written to appeal to grown-up sensibilities. The people who know, i.e., teachers, school librarians, paying-attention parents, and literary neighbors, constantly remind us that the kids in their lives won't read period unless books speak genuinely and pointedly to them (often irrespective of what we adults think children should value in children's literature).

This is not to say that grown-ups should be indiscriminate in nurturing young readers. In *Ignoramus*, Mr. Mot gives Aldo *The Indian in the Cupboard* to read because Aldo, focused as he is in this story on gender identification, thirsts for battles and blood. This funny and award-winning novel series indeed provides the masculine action Aldo craves, but as our friends at the Indian Community School in Milwaukee, Wisconsin, point out, the series also perpetuates some incendiary American Indian stereotypes. We agree with them, and we agree with Mr. Mot, because we know how imperative it is to match kids with books that speak to them and keep them reading. Plus, we're sure that Mr. Mot pulled Aldo aside for an off-camera conversation about literary typecasting. After all, it's the role of navigator, encourager, and conscience that is an adult's true calling within the world of kid lit.

Thanks to everyone who cares enough about children's literacy and literature to indulge this invective. Thanks, too, to Renée, who is instrumental in so many ways; to the Slow Sanders, who critique with impunity; to intrepid interns Guru and Jeffrey; and to Launie, Aldo's inimitable designer. And of course, to our families and Aldo's Angels we owe our inextinguishable, ineffable gratitude.

ALDO'S INIMITABLE ANGELS

Barbara Anderson

Carol & Wes Baker

Butch & Sue Byram

Michael & Pam Dobrowski

Leigh Waller Fitschen

Chris Goold

Roy Griffin

Bennett Zent and Calvin, Beckett & Camden Halvorson

Oliver Harrison (Matthew & Erin)

Terry & Theresa Harrison

Richard & Peggy Hohm

Chris Hutchinson

Vicki & Bill Krug

Papa, Tutu, Cole, Grant, Iris & Thomas Ludwin

Annette & Tom Lynch

Lisa & Kyle Miller

Kristin & Henry Mouton

The Motz & Scripps Families (McCale, Alaina, Everett, Caden, Ambria & Noah)

Jackie O'Hara & Erin Rogers

Betty Oceanak

Jackie Peterson and Emma, Dorie & Elissa

John Schiller & Suzanne Holm

Slow Sand Writers Society

Barb & Steve Spanjer

Dana Spanjer

Vince & Adrianne Tranchitella

Halo There! If you're an Aldo Zelnick fan, e-mail info@bailiwickpress.com and ask for details about becoming an Aldo's Angel. Angels receive special opportunities such as pre-publication discounts, free shipping, naming rights, and listing in the acknowledgments (especially fun for kids).

THE ALDO ZELNICK FAN CLUB IS FOR READERS OF ANY AGE WHO LOVE THE BOOK SERIES AND WANT THE INSIDE SCOOP ON ALL THINGS ZELNICKIAN.

GO TO WWW.ALDOZELNICK.COM AND CLICK ON THIS FLAG-THINGY!

SIGN UP TO RECEIVE:

- sneak preview chapters from the next book.
- an early look at coming book titles, covers, and more.
- opportunities to vote on new character names and other stuff.
- discounts on the books and merchandise.
- a card from Aldo on your birthday (for kids)!

*The Aldo Zelnick fan club is free and easy.
If you're under 13, ask your mom or dad to sign you up!*

ABOUT THE AUTHOR

Photo by Amy Fesenmaier

Karla Oceanak has been a voracious reader her whole life and a writer and editor for more than twenty years. She has also ghostwritten numerous self-help books. Karla loves doing school visits and speaking to groups about children's literacy. She lives with her husband, Scott, their three boys, and a cat named Puck in a house strewn with Legos, ping-pong balls, Pokémon cards, video games, books, and dirty socks in Fort Collins, Colorado. This is her ninth novel.

ABOUT THE ILLUSTRATOR

Kendra Spanjer divides her time between being "a writer who illustrates" and "an illustrator who writes." She decided to cultivate her artistic side after discovering that the best part of chemistry class was entertaining her peers (and her professor) with "The Daily Chem Book" comic. Since then, her diverse body of work has appeared in a number of group and solo art shows, book covers, marketing materials, fundraising events, and public places. When she invents spare time for herself to fill, Kendra enjoys skiing, cycling, exploring, discovering new music, watching trains go by, decorating cakes with her sister, making faces in the mirror, and playing with her dog, Puck.

WITH THESE STICK-ON MOUSTACHES BEE GAVE ME, I COULD TAKE CUPID SHUFFLE LESSONS INCOGNITO.*